DEDICATION

For

Steve the Slug

CONTENTS

ACKNOWLEDGMENTS

Illustrated by Maru Salem

&

Reimarie Cabalu

<u>Foreword</u>

This is a book about slugs – just in case the title wasn't clear. I am world famous for my love of slugs, my army of slugs and my appetite for slugs. Slugs are magnificent creatures and in this book you'll get to discover why, as well as meet some of my most notable slugs. If you've read *Elias Zapple's Rhymes from the Cabbage Patch* then you'll be familiar with some of my slugs already. If you haven't, then you shall be slimed. So, enter the world of slugs and enjoy. Fun and stickiness guaranteed!

<u>Steve the Slug</u>

Steve the Slug is perhaps the most famous of my slugs. He was my best mate until I accidentally killed him with my lawnmower. Steve was my top slug, closest friend, and the one that I could recite my poetry to during all hours of the night – once he listened to me for 36 hours straight and only fell asleep 28 times. He was an extremely loyal slug, standing side by side with me through thick and thin, and helping me to uncover the coup that Clyde the Slug was planning. He may not have had any special skills or superpowers (except for the normal slug traits of creating slime and being able to break into shopping centres), but he had the most important things – patience, trust, love and loyalty. How I regret choosing to mow the lawn that day, having been up all night consuming vast quantities of my patented Noggin Rocker™.

Slug Fact: Slugs have been around for millions of years.

Bob the Slug

Bob the Slug was very similar to Steve the Slug in many ways. He always listened to me, was trustworthy and very loyal. However, he was much more of a military slug, and a somewhat kamikaze one as he was always willing to put his body on the line. He didn't seem to fear anything. Bob the Slug once went skydiving without a parachute – he hadn't intended to go skydiving, I had accidentally bumped into him and he fell out of the plane… no idea how he survived. At least, Bob didn't appear to show any fear, and certainly never questioned the safety aspect when I stuck miniature sticks of dynamite on his back. In fact, that's how he met his end - carrying a powerful little bomb that accidentally went off too early, resulting in him having quite a number of final resting places.

Slug Fact: Slugs are cold-blooded.

<u>Gino the Slug</u>

Having such a muscular, well-rounded figure as mine requires a special kind of diet, and luckily I have the best slug chef in the whole world. Gino the Slug first came to me a few years ago when one day he turned up on my doorstep. He knew that I employed a number of slugs and so hoped to get a job. At the specific moment he was on my doorstep I was about to fetch my newspaper and almost trod on him. After scolding him and telling him to never just wait around on people's doorsteps, I hired him and set him to work in the kitchen.

As you can guess by his name, Gino the Slug is Italian, and therefore tends to favour Italian cuisine - for example, Spaghetti Slugonaise, Slugballs and Spaghetti, Spaghetti Slugonara, Slugagna, Grilled Slug with Pesto – he can do it all. It does tend to get a bit boring sometimes, so I do ask for a bit more variety. Being Italian, he can be quite an angry, passionate little slug, and therefore gets upset if I tell him what to cook, and starts flinging slime everywhere. At which point I pick him up and dangle him over a jar of salt. He soon gives in and goes back to being the obedient slug I require. Still, his Slugamisu is to die for.

Slug Fact: Salt sucks slugs dry.

Slug Recipe #1

<u>Slug Pie</u>

Ingredients:
- Handful of reluctant slugs.
- Rolled pastry.
- Half an onion, diced.
- One peeled potato, roughly chopped.
- Half a cup of chicken stock.

Grab your slugs then tell them that the rumours of them being in a slug pie are false, and that in fact you're taking them to go strawberry picking. As they celebrate, you give each of them a bit too much Noggin Rocker™, and when they're passing out you knock each of them on the head with a wooden mallet. Take the unconscious slugs and put them in a jar of salt. Leave them for a few hours.

Fry the onion in a pan, then when it's starting to show some colour add your salted slugs. Cook for a few minutes, add the chopped potato, and continue to fry until the potatoes are nicely browned. Add stock, and simmer for five minutes.

Take your pastry and put it into your baking dish, then pour in the slug mixture.

Cover with the rest of the pastry, and seal the top with beaten egg. Bake for 45 minutes at 180° C, then leave to stand for 5 minutes. Serve, telling your guests that it's mushroom pie.

<u>Chopper the Slug</u>

A lot of my slugs are genetically modified, as the ordinary natural slug sometimes just can't do the job. In the basement of my house I have a laboratory, where I create my very own genetically modified slugs that have some very special skills indeed. One of the first I created was Chopper the Slug. The name could give you a hint as to his special skill, as Chopper the Slug can fly like a helicopter. Helicopters are wonderful, and can fly in and out of most places making them very functional, (as they don't need runways) which is why I hit upon the idea of creating a sort of 'slug copter'. The first few didn't work out well, as merely attaching propellers to slugs doesn't work – they just fall onto the noggins of each passer-by when launched out of my bedroom window, resulting in the passer-by having to shave their noggin to rid themselves of the sticky mess. So, to the lab I went, and created a slug that grew slug-propellers. How I did this shall remain a secret, and if anybody creates a similar slug then I'll know that my secrets have been stolen!

Chopper the Slug, being an amiable, obedient slug, has proved very useful when rescuing fellow slugs from the field of combat by airlifting them out. He's also been great at landing on Dieter's noggin just to annoy him each time he goes to get his newspaper in the morning.

Slug Fact: Slugs are invertebrates, meaning they have no backbone – like Dieter.

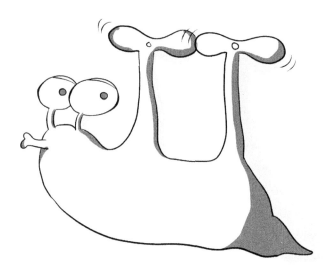

Slug Clothing

Some of my slugs require special clothing. Here are a few examples of some outfits I have designed for my slugs as modelled by Fabio the Slug:

- Casual Clothing.
- Gino the Slug's Chef's Uniform.
- Military Slug's Uniform.
- Crack Commando Slug Unit's Combat Fatigues.

Larry the Handyslug

For many of my projects – whether it's building a porch for my house or constructing a catapult so I can launch cabbages at Dieter's noggin, I needed a multi skilled slug. Therefore when Larry the Handyslug answered my ad in the local gazette, I was pleased as punch to get a carpenter/handyslug with such a wealth of practical experience. Larry the Handyslug can build anything, and is so adept that he's in demand by a number of organisations and governments. In the past he's designed numerous thrones for the Queen of England, statues like Nelson's Column, theatres like Shakespeare's Globe, and garden furniture - like the picnic table at the service station between junction 22 and junction 23 on the M25. At the moment he's constructing a slug-proof biscuit jar, so that Fatty the Slug can't get his hands on my cabbage digestives.

Slug Fact: Slugs can survive freezing weather.

<u>Fatty the Slug</u>

Fatty the Slug is a troublesome fellow, and I'm quite surprised he's still around and not yet been deep-fried and served as a slug burger. Not sure why I put up with him, as he doesn't do anything besides keep trying to get at my cabbage digestives, and breaking the occasional chair.

His weight had ballooned to 3 stone, which was enormous for a slug. Really enormous! So, my slug dieticians and I came up with a drastic work out plan for Fatty the Slug, which involved him running on a treadmill for one hour every day. The treadmill is connected to a battery that powers my entire laboratory *and* my moustache warmer. My electricity bill has never been cheaper! Fatty the Slug has since lost one stone and his will to live.

Slug Fact: Slugs can grow up to seven or eight inches in length.

General Fairfax the Slug

Having such a large army of slugs requires a general with the leadership skills of a General Eisenhower or Montgomery. Strong, stern, clear - a good speaker and motivator - one who knows how to hammer a slug into order when need be. General Fairfax the Slug is that kind of general. With numerous victories over the Snails of No. 57, the successful carpet sliming of Dieter's kitchen, and the Great Escape from the security guards at Bluewater Shopping Centre, General Fairfax the Slug has become the greatest general in slug history. Larry the Handyslug has already been commissioned to create a statue in honour of General Fairfax the Slug, which will take pride of place in my garden. The statue will be raised on a plinth, so that Dieter can see it everyday and be very annoyed. (Dieter had to have a whole new kitchen floor installed).

Slug Fact: Slugs come in almost all colours.

Slug Recipe #2

Slug Juice

Ingredients:
• Ten juicy, plump slugs.

Select the ten cleanest slugs days beforehand, the ten that are as useful as a fork made of cotton, and give them a bath every night in sugary water. Explain to them that they're being given a nightly bath for outstanding service in the field of battle, and the sugar in the water will help heal their battle-scarred bodies. When they're nice and plump, wring each one out like you would a wet towel and collect the sugary water into a cup. Enjoy.

*After being wrung dry the slugs can be re-used. However, convincing them to take sugary baths again may prove difficult.

Selina the Slug

Although my slugs and I have fought many battles with my neighbour, Dieter, (and his inferior moustache) there comes a time when battles must be fought not in the garden or with cabbages, but in courts and with lawyers. Luckily, I have the best lawyer in the slug world, Selina the Slug. She's a marvel and can outwit, outthink and outsmart the best lawyers in the world. Even though Dieter has tried to sue me multiple times and claim my slugs and my cabbages, he has yet to defeat me – thanks to Selina.

Selina came from an impoverished family of slugs, all of them hairdressers, and when she came of age and said she wanted to become a lawyer, her family were none too pleased and demanded she attend slug hairdressing school instead. Being an independent, strong-willed slug she ignored them, and went to slug law school where she excelled and was top of her class. She then went on to become the greatest ever slug lawyer. However, she never forgot her family, and successfully had them all charged with slugicide (mass slug murder) and locked up in slug prison for a very long time – even though of course they were completely innocent. Never mess with Selina the Slug.

Slug Fact: Slugs are very sensitive to wind.

Commander Jones III the Slug

Head of my Crack Commando Slug Unit is Commander Jones III the Slug. His grandfather founded the Crack Commando Slug Unit, and his father succeeded him. He then went on to further enhance the reputation of the Crack Commando Slug Unit with numerous successful missions, such as the top secret mission to find out what Dieter was using on his moustache to get it to grow to such extraordinary lengths. Commander Jones III the Slug has been able to fill the shoes of his illustrious forebears with many more successful missions, as well as overseeing combat training. Only the very elite of military slugs qualify to be a part of my Crack Commando Slug Unit.

Some have criticised Commander Jones III the Slug, saying his training and methods are too brutal – training includes spending a week alone in the Sahara Desert followed by a week at a salt mine, and only those that survive get to become part of the Crack Commando Slug Unit and get a bucketful of water.

Commander Jones III the Slug recently welcomed a new addition, his son, Jones IV the Slug, whom he hopes will follow in his, and his father's and grandfather's footsteps. If his son elects not to, then Commander Jones III the Slug has offered him up to be a part of slug stew night.

Slug Fact: Slugs have two feelers, which project from their head.

Zip, Pip and Whip the Slugs

Of course not all my slugs are military slugs, chefs or lawyers. I have a special trio of miniature slugs whose sole purpose it is to clean. They are speedy little devils that zip around my house in a nanosecond, broom, mop or duster in hand. They can get my house as spotless as a leopard that's fallen into a pool of black paint, and at such speed that Dieter has already made enquiries as to their availability – not that he'll ever get them. How I hate Dieter so!

I specially created this trio of slugs in my laboratory. I simply took away a few chromosomes here and added a few chromosomes there, including the speedy gene and the cleaner gene and hey presto, I had myself slugs to do my cleaning, which meant I could spend more time combing my moustache, Mr Snazzy.

Slug Fact: A large tiger slug can produce several teaspoons of slime a day.

Slug Recipe #3

Slug Noggin Rocker™ Stew

Ingredients:
- 500g of slugs that have been given Noggin Rocker™ nightly for at least 6 months.
- 2 potatoes.
- 1 carrot.
- 1 onion.
- Beef stock.
- Noggin Rocker™.

As your chosen stew slugs will be so disoriented thanks to the nightly consumption of Noggin Rocker™, they won't know what's happening when you add them to the pot. They'll probably think they're going for a swim. Encourage them to think that, as this will mean the slugs soaking up more flavour when swimming inside the pot. Chop your veggies, boil your stock, throw it all in with some patented Noggin Rocker™ and cook until the screams have died down. Serve with rice or eat on its own. Best not give to any hungry slugs as nobody likes eating a relative.

Gabriel and Carmen the Tango Slugs

With all this slug fighting and slug eating, you occasionally need some entertainment, and I happen to have two of the best entertainers in the slug world, Gabriel & Carmen the Tango Slugs. Hailing from Argentina, the home of the tango, they dance the tango better than anyone and leave only the tiniest little bit of slime while doing it. When they dance, my slugs and I are glued to their every graceful movement and could watch for hours on end – which sometimes happens, despite Gabriel and Carmen's resistance. They once performed for twelve hours straight, and by the end they had to be carried off on stretchers.

We've even set up a little stage and dance floor for them to perform on, and every night when they dance it's a sell-out, with slugs coming from all over the house. They're big stars here, and you quite often see slugs dressed as Gabriel and Carmen. Gabriel's attire consists of an open neck white shirt and lots of furry chest hair, and Carmen wears a bright red dress and lipstick, which complements her black wig. If you'd like tickets for their next show, then please visit www.eliaszapple.com.

Slug Fact: Slugs are gastropod molluscs.

Elias Zapple

Nobby the Slug

My slugs and I are quite into sports, and we play a wide array including cabbage throwing, cabbage bowling, Brussels sprout table tennis, cabbage ball and many others. Our favourite pastime when not watching Gabriel and Carmen dance the tango all day and night is football, and by football I mean football. Our star player is Nobby the Slug, who can do things with a football (and a cabbage) that elite human players can only dream about. Many clubs have tried to sign him and he's been quite eager to do so. The only thing standing in his way is me and a jar of salt.

When he plays he's like a magician. The way he controls the ball and the play, drifting this way and that – he's supremely gifted and runs rings around our goalkeeper Fatty the Slug - it's almost as if the ball's stuck to him (which it could well be as his slime is particularly sticky).

Whenever my slugs take on the snails at No.57 Nobby destroys them, and in the last match scored five hat tricks! Headers, bicycle kicks, scorpion kicks, diving headers, 50-yard passes – Nobby can do it all. Watching him play is so tiring it boggles the noggin, and makes me reach for my patented Noggin Rocker™. When there's no Noggin Rocker™ available I just reach for my hammer and threaten him with it so that he'll stay away, as my eyes just cannot keep up.

His relatives are pretty nifty with other sports too. His sister is a wiz at the pole vault, and can perform such high jumps that I was worried she'd one day jump the fence and escape, so I had to make her wear a hat made of iron.

Slug Fact: Slugs are very sensitive to various smells.

Chevy the Slug

As we quite often break into Dieter's home and various shopping centres, we need to know not only the layout but also if anybody's about – step forward Chevy the Slug. Chevy is another slug engineered by me, and his special skill is rather special indeed as he has the power to make himself invisible. Many slugs have pondered, and asked me the question as to whether he actually exists, as few have seen him aside from myself, Chevy himself and the late Steve the Slug. (I believe the doubt of my slugs about Chevy's existence is due to a series of missions being much more deadly than I had told them, despite my assurances that Chevy the Slug had already fully scouted the locations). However, I can assure all of you that he does exist, and has proven to be most useful when on top-secret or stealth missions, and other situations where invisibility is of the utmost importance.

Aside from being invisible, Chevy likes jazz music, mushroom pie and the colour blue. And if you don't believe that he exists, then you can see his portrait on the next page.

Slug Fact: Slugs communicate the location of food by laying slime trails.

Maren Salenl

Trevor the Slug

Trevor the Slug was one of my closest slug friends, perhaps not as close as Steve, but he was one of the slugs I felt I could recite poetry to until the wee small hours. At least I thought I could, until one day he got up and shouted, "I can't take it anymore!" and stormed off never to be seen again. He was a middle-aged slug and had been with me for many years, so his unusual outburst took all of us by surprise.

I'm man enough to admit that I wept for many days, until the tears were replaced by anger. How dare he be bored by my poetry! So I took the only course of action available, and sent my Crack Commando Slug Unit after him to finish him off. They found the traitorous slug (some American slugs have started calling him Benedict Arnold the Slug), over at Dieter's recounting what had happened. I had thought that Dieter would have sprayed Trevor with pesticide as soon as he was discovered on his property - however it seems that Dieter will sink to any level, and instead tried to secure his services.

My Crack Commando Slug Unit waited till dusk, then when Dieter had gone off to apply tonic to his inferior moustache, they came charging in and whisked Trevor the Slug away. Trevor the Slug was charged with defamation, treason and consorting with the enemy, and sentenced to death by catapult. He was then catapulted over to the Snails at No.57, where I believe he was stuck in a shell, exported to France, then cooked and served at the Ritz Hotel, Paris. Monsieur Boularot enjoyed eating his escargot (snails) so much that he personally complimented the chef.

Slug Fact: Slugs don't need calcium, unlike snails that use it to build their shell.

Slug Recipe #4

<u>Slug Cereal</u>

Ingredients:
- 15 beach-loving slugs.
- Milk.

When the sky is blue and the sun is at its strongest, take your beach-loving slugs for a day out to the seaside and give them coconut oil instead of sunscreen. When they've fallen asleep, tie them down and let them tan then burn until they're all dry and crisp like dehydrated sundried tomatoes. Add them to a bowl and pour your milk. Mmm, crunchy nutritious cereal!

Gordon the Slug

The one main weakness, the Achilles heel, of all my slugs is salt. All my enemies, (Dieter, the snails at No.57) and myself know it. (Though most of my military and Crack Commando Slug Units wear special anti-salt clothing). It is still a sure fire way to defeat my slugs, and for me to threaten my slugs, in which case salt is especially handy. However, though we can sometimes get around a salt attack, if salt is thrown then my slugs are drier than a desert and as dead as that snail I squished this morning. So, for many months I worked busily away in my lab and I finally created a slug that's immune to salt! That's right, I have a slug that could literally swim in salt and would emerge moist, slimy and eager for some vinegar. Meet Gordon the Slug.

Gordon wasn't engineered from scratch like Chopper the Slug or my infamous Creepy-Crawly (the one that eats children's heads), he was your average slug that did the odd job here and there, and attended the occasional slug convention in my hallway. So I said to Gordon, "Would you like to be more than average? Would you like to be one of the more notable slugs like General Fairfax?" He said no and carried on his way to the convention. Feeling miffed, I stroked Mr Snazzy then picked up Gordon the Slug anyway, and took him down to the laboratory and injected him with my special anti-salt concoction. I then subjected Gordon the Slug to hours of torture, by dipping him in salt and throwing salt at him; he was not at all happy. It was worth it, however, as he emerged unscathed and moist as ever.

Since that day, Gordon the Slug has been one of the vanguard (leaders) in various missions, and awarded the Elias Zapple medal for bravery numerous times. Gordon the Slug is also lucky in another away – I will never eat him, as it's impossible to make him flavourful.

Slug Fact: Slug slime, the mucous, enables the slug to move and also acts as a brake.

Elias Zapple

50

Akira the Ninja Slug

When planning military attacks and being involved in slug-to-snail combat, it's important to be familiar with and the master of many different fighting styles. Fortunately, my slugs are trained in a number of ways from traditional combat techniques such as boxing, wrestling and sliming, as well as those styles from cabbage patches further afield, specifically Japan. Meet Akira the Ninja Slug, master of Ninjitsu – the Japanese art of stealth, camouflage and sabotage. Not only does Akira train many of my slugs, some of which have graduated and formed a special Ninja Slug Unit, (headed by Akira), but he has also voluntarily assisted in many missions himself. Using stealth and camouflage he has infiltrated the snail's cabbage patch at No. 57, entered Dieter's home on more than one occasion, and managed to extract numerous bags of salt and vinegar crisps from the supermarket when they closed early one evening.

Akira's easy to spot, when he's not in stealth mode, as he always wears his ninja outfit, and can quite often be seen fishing in my pond prior to preparing sashimi dishes. I don't particularly like sashimi, so I give every plate of it to the Creepy-Crawly. I'm not sure if the

Creepy-Crawly likes it either. However, if he doesn't eat it then he'll starve so he has no choice… unless one day I forget to lock his cage door.

Akira also enjoys riding ponies.

Slug Fact: Slugs do not have a proper brain.

Goldie the Slug

Goldie the Slug is not a Labrador slug, he is in fact a slug with gold teeth. Why does he have gold teeth? Because he's quite a wealthy slug, and he's into all things bling such as flashy, baggy clothes, a gold clock around his neck, his hair shaped in various ways (at the moment it's in the shape of a 50 pence coin), a bouncing red convertible car, and many slugettes that always hang around with him. For you see, Goldie's a rapper, and every day he swaggers around rapping about this and that. He'll rap about cabbages, rap about me, rap about Fatty the Slug, rap about the cost of slug feeds – you name it, he'll rap about it.

Goldie can out rap anybody, as he did to Sloopy Sloop the Snail whom Goldie beat so badly at a previous rap battle that Sloopy Sloop had to be put on life support. Sloopy Sloop the Snail died soon afterwards, when Akira sneaked into his hospital room to steal the cupcakes his snail comrades had given him, and accidentally pulled the plug out from the socket.

And here's a bit of the rap that destroyed Sloopy Sloop the Snail:

'Straight outta slug land, a zany slug called
Goldie
From the group run by the moustachioed oldie
When I'm called up, I let slime off
Squeeze my body and snails are hauled off
You too, Sloopy, if you try to mess with me
Zapple's gonna have to come and get me
Off your shell, that's how I'm going out
Cos I'm gonna come and knock you out
Slugs start to mumble, they want to rumble
Mix them and cook them in a pot like gumbo
Going off on a snail that fell
With slime that's aimed at your shell…'

There's a lot more to the rap, however Goldie has refused to give me further permission to print any more. I have also gotten quite hungry after 'gumbo' was mentioned, and so now I'll go and see whether Gino the Slug can make a Slug Gumbo for tonight's dinner.

Slug Fact: A slug's feelers will regrow if cut off.

Alice the Slug

Alice the Slug is a guitar legend. The best guitarist since Emma the Guitarist, and certainly better than Fillmore. Alice the Slug can often be found atop of Slug Hill, playing his Les Slug guitar for hours on end as the wind breezes through his long black hair. He truly is a guitar legend, and looks the part too and not just because of his long hair. He wears a trademarked black top hat, black T-shirt, and like all rock guitarists he enjoys eating gummy slugs (like gummy bears but slugs, not bears).

He often demands that a spotlight be fixed upon him, (which has to soon be removed as he starts to sizzle) and then get ready as he goes through his set of classic rock songs, such as:

1. Drive My Slug.
2. Enter Sandslug.
3. Slug on the Water.
4. Smells Like Slug Spirit.
5. Bohemian Slugsody.
6. While My Slug Gently Weeps.
7. Iron Slug.
8. Paranoid Slugroid.
9. Sweet Slug O'Mine.
10. Whole Lotta Slug.

There are many, many others that he plays, sometimes for the whole night, at which point I'm forced to command Commander Jones III the Slug and his Crack Commando Slug Unit to unplug Alice the Slug's guitar, then slugnap Alice and torture him by tying him down and forcing him to listen to one of Goldie the Slug's raps about the cost of slug feeds. Alice the Slug no longer plays for entire nights, and I'm now able to get a peaceful night's sleep.

Slug Fact: Slugs play a vital role in maintaining a healthy ecosystem by consuming decaying vegetation, dead leaves and dead flesh!

Quiz

1. Which slug powers my laboratory?
2. Which slug was killed by a lawnmower?
3. What's the profession of Selina the Slug?
4. Which dance are Gabriel & Carmen the Slugs famous for?
5. What special power does Chevy the Slug have?
6. Who founded my Crack Commando Slug Unit?
7. How did Bob the Slug die?
8. How many grams of slug should one use when making Slug Noggin Rocker™ Stew?
9. Who has the better moustache, Dieter, or the great Elias Zapple?
10. Where is the picnic table Larry the Handyslug made?
11. Which food does Akira the Ninja Slug like to prepare?
12. What's the Achilles' heel of most slugs?
13. What kind of guitar does Alice the Slug play?

Elias Zapple's Book of Slugs

Answers: 1) Fatty the Slug. 2) Steve the Slug. 3) Lawyer. 4) The tango. 5) Invisibility. 6) Commander Jones the Slug. 7) A bomb he carried accidentally went off. 8) 500g. 9) Elias Zapple. 10) Between junctions 22 & 23 on the M25.11) Sashimi. 12) Salt. 13) Les Slug.

Elias Zapple

The Unlikely Story of Elias Zapple

Elias Zapple was not born in 1922, as some would have you believe. His date of birth is not really relevant anyway. What *is* relevant is that he arose out of a tulip that was growing in some old granny's garden in Camberwell. How he got to be in a tulip is not really clear, nor is it clear how he got out of the tulip, and years later wrote the smash hit musical, *'Love, be a Stranger'*, which was an international flop.

After that success, he went on to work as a 19th century Victorian chimney sweep, when he was inspired to write the acclaimed series of books entitled *'Duke & Michel'*. It is believed the fumes from the chimneys did so much damage to Elias, that it was a miracle he ever ate a cupcake again.

Later, he travelled back in time to the present, and went on a series of trips to many foreign and distant lands. During these travels, Elias met and listened to many interesting people, choosing to ignore all of them. He did, however, learn a couple of things: i) the earth is flat; and ii) you should never eat a banana when it's not ripe.

Many questions are often asked by his adoring public. Are you human? How many chimpanzees can fit inside a fridge? What is that thing growing on the side of your head? To which Mr Zapple has always smiled, turned away and swum off into the sunset; having only once been bitten by an unfriendly shark.

Elias Zapple continues to work towards the unification of Korea, and writing children's stories that parents will spend huge sums of money on. He wishes you all to know that every penny made from the books will go straight into his bank account, which he will then spend on a lavish, new tent.

For more useless information about Elias Zapple, please visit:
www.eliaszapple.com

Also by Elias Zapple

The Mysterious Corridor
The King Tingaling Painting
Return of the Nibbles

Jellybean the Dragon
Cyril the Dragon
Fillmore the Dragon

Fangless
Big Fangs
Blood, Blood Everywhere
Dead Again

A Christmas Carol… Slimed

Elias Zapple's Rhymes from the Cabbage Patch
Elias Zapple's Book of Slugs
Elias Zapple's Book of Slugs Colouring Book

Printed in Great Britain
by Amazon